MYSTERY of the MISSING WIGS

Written by Janet Palazzo-Craig
Illustrated by Paul Harvey

Troll Associates

Library of Congress Cataloging in Publication Data

Palazzo-Craig, Janet.
    Mystery of the missing wigs.

    (A Troll easy-to-read mystery)
    Summary: When their neighbor loses her
fanciful wigs and an emerald necklace, two foxy
sleuths tackle the case.
    [1. Animals—Fiction.   2. Mystery and detective
stories]   I. Harvey, Paul, 1926-   ill.
II. Title.   III. Series: Troll easy-to-read
mystery.
PZ7.P1762My   [Fic]   81-7615
ISBN 0-89375-592-3   AACR2
ISBN 0-89375-593-1 (pbk.)

MYSTERY of the MISSING WIGS

It was a quiet evening at 227 Woodbine Road.

Everything was quite cozy. Elwood R. Fox, Esquire, was lighting a fire in the fireplace. "Look at that blaze, dear," he called to his wife, Hollyhocks. She looked up from the book she was reading. "Very nice, dear," she said.

Their two children were in the den. Sly was practicing his saxophone. His little sister, Sally, sat on the floor. She was playing with her pet chicken, Cluck. Sly thought Cluck was dumb.

"Keep that Cluck away from me," said Sly.

"Go blow your horn," said Sally.

"*Sisters!*" thought Sly. He had just begun the first notes of "Swinging on a Star," when there was a loud knock at the front door. Then another, and another.

"Who can that be at this hour?" said Elwood. He opened the door. There stood Ruthy Rabbit, their next-door neighbor.

Ruthy was a fancy dresser. She was wrapped in a thick coat of white fur. She was wearing dark sunglasses with sparkles on the rims. Ruthy also wore diamond earrings—three pairs of them, for her ears were quite long. She looked very glamorous, except for one thing. Her hair was a mess. Usually, Ruthy wore a wig of blond curls—or red curls—or long, black hair. Ruthy had quite a lot of wigs. But today her hair looked awful.

All in all, Elwood was not too surprised to see Ruthy. Ruthy had a way of showing up. And when she did, it was always with news. And the news was never good.

"Goodness gracious! I *had* to tell you!
I just don't know what to do!" Ruthy said.
"They're gone—gone, I tell you. And so is
the necklace. Nowhere to be found. I shall
tear out my hair!"

Ruthy went on and on. By now, all the Foxes had come into the hallway to see what was going on.

"I shall tear out my hair ..." continued Ruthy.

"If I may make a suggestion," interrupted Elwood, politely, "I don't believe that tearing out your hair will do one bit of good. Now come inside and tell us what exactly is the problem. Begin at the beginning." Elwood could be very logical at times.

They seated Ruthy in front of the fire.
Everyone gathered around her.

"I came right over to warn you! There is a thief in our midst," began Ruthy. "I was to tea today at Madame Miranda Panda's. The most awful thing happened. Her emerald necklace is missing. It was taken almost before our eyes."

18

The Foxes were speechless. They knew of the beautiful necklace and its rich owner, Miranda Panda.

"But that's not the worst of it," continued Ruthy. "The worst of it is that someone has taken all of my wigs—every last one! The blond one, the curly one, the long, black one, the short one, and the red one, too! Who would want my wigs?"

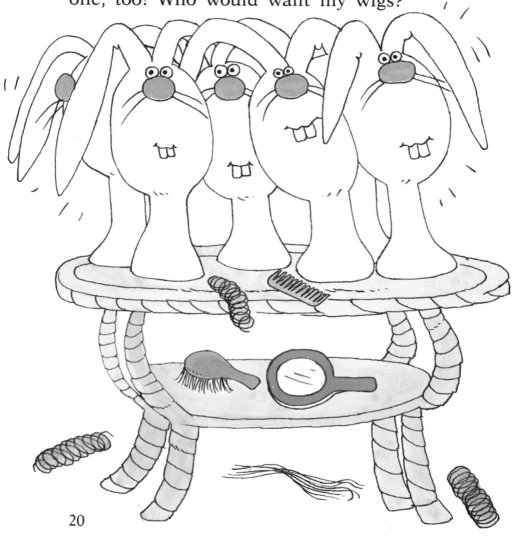

Elwood raised his eyebrows. The little
Foxes raised their eyebrows. "Who,
indeed?" asked Elwood.

The Foxes didn't have any wigs – or
any emeralds, for that matter. So they
weren't *too* worried. But that night, they
did lock up everything extra tight. Sly put
his saxophone in a special hiding place.
And Sally kept Cluck in a basket right
next to her bed.

The next morning, Sly was awakened
by a squawk. It was Cluck.

"Shut that dumb Cluck up!" said Sly.

"Go sit on an egg," said Sally. "Wake
up. Let's figure out a way to find the
emerald necklace."

"And Ruthy's wigs!" Sly added.

The little Foxes went outside to the small chicken coop behind the house. No chickens lived in the coop anymore. They had all disappeared a long time ago. Except, of course, for Cluck.

Sally and Sly made a sign. They hung
it on the door of the coop. It said:
PRIVATE! DETECTIVES AT
WORK—KEEP OUT!!

"Who do you think would want to take a necklace and a bunch of wigs?" asked Sally.

"I don't know," said Sly. "But if anyone can find out—*we* can!"

All day, they planned and plotted. They plotted and planned. They only came outside for lunch—gooseberry-and-peanut-butter sandwiches with milk. Detective work was a hungry business.

That night, Hollyhocks and Elwood
tucked their children into bed. Hollyhocks
sat down and opened her book. Elwood
put a record on the phonograph.

The moon rose high over all the houses on Woodbine Road. By and by, Sly heard a little squawk. It was Sally's chicken. "Come on, let's go," whispered Sally.

On tiptoes, the little Foxes, with Cluck close behind them, sneaked down the back steps. Under the moonlight, they trotted along until they came to Miranda Panda's mansion. Inch by inch, they tiptoed closer.

"Squawk!" said Cluck. Sly jumped
five inches off the ground.

"Quiet!" he hissed. "Let's look in the
window."

They poked their noses over the
windowsill. Inside was a most grand sight.
Music played. Dancers danced. Candles
twinkled from the ceilings and walls. It
was Madame Miranda Panda's Annual
Ball.

The Foxes sneaked inside. They crawled under a table. Their noses peeked from under the lace tablecloth.

"Do you see who I see?" asked Sally.

"She sure gets around," said Sly.

For there, dressed in a white fur coat and wearing sunglasses with sparkles on the rims, was Ruthy Rabbit. But her hair wasn't a mess anymore. She was wearing a wig of long, black hair. She was wearing three pairs of earrings, too. But somehow her ears looked different.

Suddenly, Cluck flew out from under
the table. He flew straight at Ruthy's ears,
squawking loudly the whole time.

Ruthy clutched at her ears. But something strange happened. One of the ears fell right off. *Crash,* to the floor, earrings and all.

Sly and Sally rushed out from beneath the tablecloth. Sly picked up the ear. "This is *not* a rabbit's ear," he announced. Everyone, including Miranda Panda, had gathered around by this time. "And this," said Sally, "is not Ruthy Rabbit." She pulled at the long, black hair and off it came.

There stood the famous thief, Sticky Claws Jay. Sticky Claws was a jailbird known far and wide for his clever disguises. But now, standing there with one ear on and one ear off, he looked more than a bit foolish. His blue tail feathers stuck out from beneath the white coat. His handbag was packed with stolen jewels. "Curses upon you!" cried Sticky Claws, pointing to Sally and Sly. "And a pox on that drat chicken!"

"You clever Foxes," exclaimed Miranda. "You have found the thief! We must celebrate." As they led Sticky Claws away, everyone agreed that a party to honor Sally and Sly (and Cluck, too, of course) should be held.

The next night, there was dancing and singing and plenty to eat. Everyone was invited. Ruthy Rabbit—the *real* Ruthy— was there. And this time, she was wearing a curly red wig. For back at Sticky Claws' nest, they had found the rest of Ruthy's wigs, and the emerald necklace, too.

Miranda Panda made a very nice speech. She thanked Sally and Sly for catching the thief. Everyone cheered. Elwood and Hollyhocks were proud.

"Goodness gracious," said Ruthy, as she rushed over to Sly and Sally. "I must thank you for helping to find my wigs. To think that scoundrel thought he could get away with such a thing! But how did you figure out who the thief was?"

"It wasn't hard—" said Sly.

"You might say we owe it all to the luck of a Cluck," said Sally.